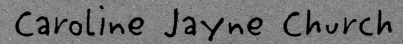

Caroline Jayne Church

RUFF!

and the
Wonderfully
Amazing
Busy Day

text by
Gillian Shields

HARPER

An Imprint of HarperCollinsPublishers

Ruff! and the Wonderfully Amazing Busy Day
Copyright © 2013 by Caroline Jayne Church
All rights reserved. Manufactured in China.
For information address HarperCollins Children's Books, a division of
HarperCollins Publishers, 10 East 53rd Street, New York, NY 10022.
www.harpercollinschildrens.com

Library of Congress Cataloging-in-Publication Data is available.
ISBN 978-0-06-201498-6 (trade bdg.)

Typography by Jeanne L. Hogle
13 14 15 16 17   SCP   10 9 8 7 6 5 4 3 2 1

First Edition

For little Max

—C.J.C.

Ruff was a busy dog.

He dug like dogs do,

pulling up the weeds

and planting pretty flowers in his backyard.

"Busy, busy, all day long,
toodle-oodle, that's my song!"

Ruff hummed cheerfully as he washed the window of his house.
Then he polished the doorknob and swept the step. Another job done!
Ruff stopped singing. Sometimes he thought it would be nicer if
there was someone else to sing with him. . . .

Ruff jumped up, ready to get busy again. There was a grassy, muddy, messy place near the apple tree.

"I know!" said Ruff. "I'll make a pond. That's just what the backyard needs."

It was hard work, digging the hole to make a pond, but Ruff didn't mind hard work. He was digging up an especially big rock when . . .

"Help!" cried a squeaky voice. A tiny gray mouse rolled out of the grass at Ruff's feet.

"What's the matter?" asked Ruff.

"Someone has dug up my Hubble house," cried the mouse.

Ruff quickly hid the shovel behind his back.

"What's a Hubble house?" he asked.

"I am Hubble," said the mouse, "and that was my house."

Ruff's happy busy feeling disappeared. He had ruined Hubble's house! And he hadn't even known that a mouse lived in his backyard!

Hubble was packing up.

"Where are you going?" cried Ruff.

"To look for a new house," Hubble replied. "Good-bye!"

"No! Wait! Stop!"

Ruff ran around in circles and did somersaults to get Hubble's attention.

He crash-landed in the flower bed.

"I'll make you another house! Please stay!"
"Really?" said Hubble.
"Really and truly."

Ruff rushed over to the shed. He found some wood, some nails, a hammer, and a can of paint. He was tremendously busy for a long time.

"Is it ready yet?" asked Hubble.
"Not yet. Ouch!" Ruff banged his paw with the hammer. "Don't worry! Almost finished!"

Hubble found ways to pass the time.
He did his exercises . . .

he did his knitting . . .

then he played his trumpet.
Finally . . .

The new Hubble house was ready!

"It's perfect!" said Hubble. "You are amazing."

"So are you," said Ruff shyly. "Please play your trumpet again."

"Don't you think we should clean up first?" said Hubble.

"Clean up?" said Ruff. "Oh, right, the pond!"

He had forgotten about it. There was mud and muck everywhere and a half-finished hole.

"I'll help you," said Hubble, putting away his trumpet and his knitting. So Ruff and Hubble worked together, digging and shoveling and filling the pond with water. And as they worked they sang.

"Busy, busy, all day long, wiggle-squiggle, that's our song!"

Ruff was very happy. The pond was beautiful, just what the backyard needed. And now he had Hubble to sing with too. What an amazing day! Ruff couldn't think of anything else he could wish for when . . .

SPLASH!

Something small and yellow and feathery tumbled from the sky
and landed right in the new pond!
It was an angry little duck.

She swam around in circles, squawking and spluttering and waggling her wings.

"Hello!" said Ruff. "Who are you?"

The duck stopped swimming for a minute. "My name is Lottie, and if anyone is rude to me, I'll . . . I'll . . . explode!"

"Please don't explode," said Hubble. "What's the matter? And why would I be rude to you?"

"Well," said Lottie, ruffling her feathers. "The other ducks were flying to a new home on the Big River. They said I was too small to fly all that way with them. Too small! Me? Ridiculous!"

"Well, you are pretty small," whispered Hubble.

"Not as small as a mouse." Lottie glared.

"So what happened?" asked Ruff.

Lottie hung her head. "I got tired. My wings ached so much that I began to fall. I guess they were right. I was too small." And she burst into noisy, quacky tears.

Ruff felt so sorry for Lottie that he ran around trying to find things to cheer her up.

He brought her a bone, a sun hat, a water balloon, and a bowl of popcorn.

He tried giving her a necklace and a flower and a half-eaten sausage, but she just cried and cried.

"And now I have nowhere to live!"

Lottie sobbed.

Ruff looked at Hubble.
Hubble looked at Ruff.
They both had a brilliant idea.

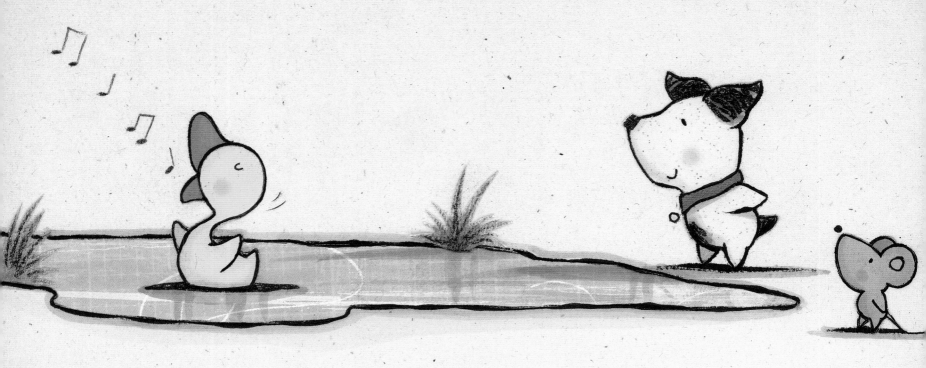

"You can live here with us!" they shouted.

"Here?" said Lottie.

"In our new pond," said Ruff excitedly.

Lottie sniffed. She inspected the pond carefully. She swam around in circles and flapped her wings. She began to sing.

"Swimming, swimming, all day long, splashy-splishy, that's my song!"

"So you'll stay?" asked Hubble.

"Please!" Ruff begged. "A small pond needs a small duck!"

"You're right," said Lottie happily.

That night, when Ruff went to bed, he called out, "Good night, Hubble! Good night, Lottie!"

When his new friends answered, "Good night, Ruff," he wanted to sing and stand on his head and do somersaults.

It had been the most wonderfully amazing busy day. And the best thing was that in the morning, Ruff and Hubble and Lottie would still be together . . .

. . . ready for tomorrow.